Love Person

by Aditi Brennan Kapil

A SAMUEL FRENCH ACTING EDITION

SAMUEL
FRENCH
FOUNDED 1830

NEW YORK HOLLYWOOD LONDON TORONTO

SAMUELFRENCH.COM

MUSIC USE NOTE

IMPORTANT BILLING AND CREDIT REQUIREMENTS

LOVE PERSON was developed and received its world premiere at Mixed Blood Theatre, Minnesota (Jack Reuler, artistic director) as part of the National New Play Network's Continued Life for New Plays Program on February 29, 2008. The performance was directed by Risa Brainin, assistant director was Sara Rademacher, with sets by Nayna Ramey, costumes by Christine Richardson, lighting by Michael Klaers, sound by C. Andrew Mayer, props by Gwen Heyn, and projections design by Nayna Ramey and Michael Klaers. The ASL Signmaster was Raymond Luczak, theASL Interpreter was Rachel Arth, the production manager was Rainbow S. Plant, the stage manager was Julia Gallagher and the dramaturg was Liz Engelman. The cast was as follows:

VIC	Jennifer Maren
FREE	Alexandria Wailes
MAGGIE	Erin McGovern
RAM	Rajesh Bose

CHARACTERS

VIC – 30s, two divorces, drinks too much. Free's sister. Some basic ASL skills. – Brash

FREE – 30s-40s, Deaf, Maggie's lover, Vic's older sister. Uses ASL exclusively, does not voice. – Restless

MAGGIE – 30s-40s, English Lit professor, Free's lover. Fluent ASL, interpreting for Free is second nature. When they're alone together they sign only. – Content

RAM (pronounced "Raahm") – Sanskrit Professor from East Coast, Second generation, fully westernized. Here on a short visit, quiet and intelligent. – Lonely

SET

On the back wall is a large screen where all email communications and telephone calls are displayed, also the dialogue of scenes that are ASL only, as specified.

If your production opts for ASL access, as opposed to screen access, for the scenes between Vic and Ram...

A streetlight where Maggie interprets the scenes between Vic and Ram into ASL, and where Free performs the ASL poems in Parts 2 and 3. The streetlight provides a heightened reality where Free and Maggie connect with their memories of the past, and their present day fascinations with Ram and Vic, while at the same time providing bilingual access.

SOUND

The qualities of sound and silence are important elements in this play.

Vic's world (i.e. the club) is noisy, drunk, and full of people. By contrast Free's world (her home with Maggie) is silent. Ram's home is quiet, though not necessarily silent. How noisy or quiet the characters are supports the connections they make, Free and Ram have quiet in common, Maggie and Vic both have a need for some noise.

The poems opening parts 2 and 3 relate to Free and Ram, and should be just the Sanskrit and ASL in conversation with each other with no extraneous sound. At its most basic level, this play is a love story between ASL and Sanskrit.

The poems opening parts 1 and 4 relate to Ram and Vic, so sound may leak in from Vic's world; e.g., club music in part 1.

More traditional sound design does have a place in, for instance, transitions, and Ram and Free's email correspondences. Piano music (like typing, like snow) may be suitable.

READING THE SCRIPT

Roman .... Spoken English

[Roman] .... ASL

[<u>Roman</u>] .... Spoken English and ASL

(Italic) .... Stage Directions

(On screen: projections*)* .... On screen communication

PRIMARY SPEAKER/VOICER OR INTERPRETER ..... for instance marks
when Maggie interprets

ACKNOWLEDGEMENTS

The playwright would like to thank the following people for their invaluable contributions to this play:

Deaf performer Nicole Zapko for her inspiring work as an artist, and for her advice and input throughout the writing of this play,

Lisa Zapko for her tireless interpreting, and her wise insights,

Satish Kapil for the conversations about poetry and Sanskrit,

Jack Reuler for providing an artistic home in Mixed Blood Theatre,

Liz Engelman for the dramaturgy and friendship,

Sandy Shinner, and Victory Gardens Theatre, for assistance acquiring the cover art and sanskrit transcriptions.

Sean Brennan, my love person.

PART I

Scene One

(RAM's voice in dark reciting verse from Srngara-tilaka, verse appears on screen in Sanskrit script.)

(During the V.O., lights fade up on VIC and RAM in Vic's apartment, dimly lit, throbbing music. VIC laughs and moves to the music, eyes closed, glass of red wine in hand. RAM watches her, fascinated, aroused. Lights fade out.)

RAM. *(V.O.)*

Aviditasukhaduhkham nirgunam vastu kincit
Jadamatir iha kascin moksa ityacacakse
Mama tu matam anangasmerata runyaghurnan –
Madakalamadir aksi – nivimokso hi moksah

(Lights up on RAM speaking at a nightclub, similar throbbing music turned down low. No one really showed up, it's awkward, but he finishes a snippet of the poem and then reads the translation. VIC, FREE and MAGGIE watch from a table, MAGGIE tries to interpret the poem into ASL for FREE. ASL is not on screen.)

RAM.	MAGGIE.
...Madakalamadiraksi – nuvimokso hi moksah	[wait...Sanskrit... Sanskrit...]
OK, so in English...	[OK, now English –]
Some in this world insist	[People think]
That a certain whatever	[something... what-
– it – is	ever...]

That has no taste of   [no joy no sad]
Joy or sorrow   [lost people]
No qualities   **FREE.**
Is Release   [Which people?]
They are fools   **MAGGIE.**

                                   [The people who think
                                   they're 'lost']
To my mind her   **FREE.**
Body unfurling   [What does that mean,
                                   'lost'?]

With joy of being young   **MAGGIE.**
Flowering out of love   [It's poetry, wait, let me
                                   understand it]
Her eyes floating as   **VIC.**
with wine and
Words wandering with   [Pay attention!]
love
Then the undoing of the
knot
Of her sari
That   **MAGGIE.**
Is Release

                                   [Ok, ok –]
                                   [When young lovers,
                                   their clothes off]
                                   [drunk, chatting, that is
                                   letting go –]
                                   [Shit! Sorry. Did you get
                                   anything from that?]
                          FREE.

                                   (laughing) [That
                                   sucked!]

*(**RAM** finishes, **VIC** claps enthusiastically. Out of sight there is hooting and hollering from busboys and waitresses – "Yeah, Ram!" "Not bad man!" "Wooo…" embarrassed, **RAM** exits toward the ruckus, muttering 'Shut up.')*

(Thumping club music amps up almost immediately, remains throughout the scene. Meanwhile...)

(ASL is not on screen.)

MAGGIE.	VIC.
[I know, I'm sorry! I know I can do better, hold on,] [let me try to summarize...]	Whadya think, huh? That was [<u>good</u>], right?

FREE.

    [I have no clue]

VIC.	MAGGIE.
[<u>What? No!</u>]	[<u>My fault! That was terrible, interpreter malfunction big time</u>]

FREE.	VIC.
[That's ok, it don't think it's my style]	Shit man, I really wanted you to hear it!

MAGGIE.

    [<u>Well it might have been your style if I hadn't screwed it up</u>]

VIC.

    Know what? I'll [<u>go get him</u>], he can do it [<u>again</u>], [<u>you're gonna love it,</u>] I swear, he's a total sweetheart! Maggie will rock it this time!

(VIC exits.)

Hey Ram! Woooo, that rocked!

(beat)

(ASL on screen)

FREE. [She's sleeping with him]

MAGGIE. [So?]

FREE. ["Oh hey, let's do something different, there's a poetry reading at the club, come on, it'll be fun – "]

MAGGIE. [Well, that was mostly true]

FREE. [Maybe she'll marry him – lucky #3.]

[How much do you want to bet she forgets about us and doesn't come back?]

MAGGIE. [She's coming back. Stop being such a big sister, you're too judgmental – try to have some fun]

(VIC and RAM enter, RAM is still holding the poem. He is courteous, but would like to leave.)

(ASL not on screen)

VIC. OK, so [Ram], this is my [sister] Free, also Jones, and her [partner] Maggie Etulain

RAM./MAGGIE. [Hello, hello, pleased to meet you, I feel like an idiot]

VIC. Nooo!

MAGGIE. That was a lovely reading, thank you!

RAM./MAGGIE. No, thank you, for showing up –

[– though the busboys found me fascinating, I'm sure!]

MAGGIE. [Oh, actually, is that the poem? May I see it?]

RAM. Sure, did I butcher it that badly?

(RAM hands the poem to MAGGIE.)

MAGGIE. No, no, I did…

(FREE snatches the poem.)

FREE.

(to MAGGIE) [I'll just read it]

MAGGIE.

[You sure?]

MAGGIE. […I butchered it, and I was feeling badly about it, so –]

(silent beat as they watch FREE read)

VIC. OK, so you want a [drink]? On me!

RAM./MAGGIE. [No, thanks, I… I'll pass.]
[I get dehydrated on airplanes]

VIC. Aw, poor baby

RAM./MAGGIE. [I should probably go get my bags. You can hang on to that if you'd like –]

VIC. Hey, no, no, you've got time, siddown!

RAM./MAGGIE. [Well, just a little bit, I like to be early – but I guess my ride's not here yet –]

VIC. That's right, [so kick back], [enjoy] the last few minutes of your vacation!

(Beat. **MAGGIE** *tries to make conversation.)*

MAGGIE. [Did you translate this poem? From the original?]

RAM./MAGGIE. [No, not at all, I don't do that sort of thing. This guy, Merwin, he's planning a book and the head of our department is collaborating, he wrote this one –]
[It's the best translation I've come across, which is not saying much.]
[Then again, it all sounds wrong to me once it leaves Sanskrit, so I'm a poor judge –]

*(***FREE*** *is done with the poem, hands the paper back.)*

RAM./MAGGIE. [What do you think?]

FREE./MAGGIE. [Hard to say]

RAM. Ah

MAGGIE. It's hard to translate English to ASL, especially poetry.

VIC. [Maggie teaches] poetry too!

RAM.	**FREE.**
Oh?	[Can we leave?]

MAGGIE.	VIC.
[Yes. Yes.]	[No! Stay!]
[Which is why I was par-	
ticularly embarrassed]	
[To do such a poor job	FREE.
of interpreting it. Um.]	
[So, tell me more about	[Why??]
this poem,]	
[It was great!]	

RAM./MAGGIE. [Oh, it's ancient. Most of my work is. I
didn't know what to read – then I thought maybe
a thematic sort of tie – in, wine, bar, intoxication
and, I don't know –]
[Anyway, thanks. It was alright.]

VIC. You [kicked ass], I shit you not! And Maggie is like
my [smartest friend], she knows poetry, and she
loved it! – so come on, relaaax…

(VIC kisses RAM, it's awkward.)

VIC. Don't be shy! Are you shy? [He's shy]!

RAM.	FREE./MAGGIE.
[No, I'm not shy]	[How did you two
	meet?]

VIC. I just [picked him up] after my shift last Thursday

RAM./MAGGIE. [I'm visiting	
my cousin Birju, the	
asshole who talked me	
into doing this reading	
and then didn't have	
the good grace to stick	
around to laugh at me.]	FREE.
He better still be plan-	[He doesn't like that
ning to take me to the	poem?]
airport, where is he?	

FREE./MAGGIE. [(Um, Free is asking)] – You don't like
it?

RAM. What?

MAGGIE. Your poem.

RAM./MAGGIE. [No, I do! I'm sorry, I didn't mean to sound… It's one of my favorites actually.]

[Just, in English, what's the difference really? It's some foreign thing that you're hearing, a novelty…though I'm delighted of course if you liked it… ah…]

[I'm sorry, is there a protocol? Stupid question – should I speak slower so you can – ?]

MAGGIE. [No, I'm fine. You can speak at your normal pace. You don't like translations?]

RAM./MAGGIE. [Hate them!]

VIC. Hey!

RAM./MAGGIE. [Hate them hate them hate them, they make me feel stupid]

VIC. Well, I love this poem! I'm [keeping] it!

MAGGIE. [I thought it was lovely –]

VIC.

[This is our poem!]

(FREE gives MAGGIE a look.)

I'm [gonna frame it]!
And, plus, handy letterhead – so I can
[call you]! Or, hey, email you.]
Or, better still – fax!

MAGGIE.
  [What?]

FREE.
  [How do you know it's beautiful?]

(They look at FREE & MAGGIE)
Guys?

MAGGIE.
  [I'm just saying I think it is]

FREE.
  [But you don't know]

MAGGIE. [Sorry! This is an ongoing debate for us. Practical concerns of daily life aside, Free would rather not bother with English. Which I find unrealistic –]

(FREE interrupts.)

FREE. [Ask what his poem really says]

MAGGIE. Free is asking – [What does your poem really say?]

RAM./MAGGIE. [How do you mean?]

FREE./MAGGIE. [Just the words, what are all the words?]

(beat)

RAM./MAGGIE. [Oh great, now I'm going to if possible sound even more idiotic.]

[Ok, it's something like –]

(He gets a little comical with it.)

[Foolish man – joy or pain in material things – worthless! Salvation!]

[My opinion – uncovering… art of love intoxication – loosening the waistband – salvation!]

[You see, it's nonsense.]

[I have to tell you though, that I find everything clearer in Sanskrit. It's more precise, simpler.]

[What is true release, true love – it's hard to explain in any language, right? But I think Sanskrit succeeds… or comes closer anyway…]

[Do you know it's at the root of most Indo – European languages? You're all speaking Sanskrit right now, just in an incredibly impure form.]

VIC. Yeah?

RAM./MAGGIE. [Yes… say something –]

VIC. Say…? Like what?

RAM. Anything. Really.

VIC. Um. Hi, [my name is Vic], I'm a Sagittarius?

RAM./MAGGIE. Sanskrit for name is naama.

VIC. No shit!

RAM. Absolutely none.

VIC. That is so cool! *(to* **MAGGIE***)* Ok, that was mine, now you go!

RAM./MAGGIE. [Go is GAM!]

VIC. Sweet! Who the hell knows shit like that?

RAM./MAGGIE. [Thank you, that's my only party trick, I'm finished.]

*(***VIC** *laughs a lot.)*

FREE.	**RAM./MAGGIE.**
[Calm down –]	[Anyway, to me English muddies things, over-complicates them.]
VIC.	
[What?]	[Particularly Sanskrit love poetry, which needs to have a more visceral impact.]
FREE.	[I think.]
[You're like a hyperac-tive puppy]	
VIC.	
[Fuck you]	

FREE. *(interrupting* **MAGGIE***)* [I want to ask him a question. You said we are all speaking Sanskrit?]

MAGGIE. [(Free is asking)] You said we're all speaking Sanskrit?

RAM./MAGGIE. [Yes! It's just the roots of certain words,] that's where you can track it...

FREE./MAGGIE. [I'm (Free's) not speaking Sanskrit]

RAM./MAGGIE. [No, of course not, but your signing has its basis in English –]

FREE./MAGGIE. [No]

*(***MAGGIE** *tries to cover the awkwardness.)*

MAGGIE. [...but I suppose if you're not really using ASL, if you're signing more English, that could be related... distantly...]

(**FREE** *catches her attention.*)

FREE. [I'm still talking]

FREE./MAGGIE. [(Sorry) You're talking about the sounds of words, right?]

RAM./MAGGIE. [Yes]

FREE./MAGGIE. [Then ASL has no Sanskrit root. In fact, you could say that gestures, which are the actual root of ASL, came before Sanskrit.]
[Am I right?]

(*beat*)

RAM./MAGGIE. [Sure. That's very interesting. What an interesting thought.]

FREE./MAGGIE. [I think English is a very confusing language. I feel bad for hearing people.]
[Like you two, for instance, how would you describe your relationship? Dating, flirting, interested, long distance relationship? Don't know?]
[So many words, very little meaning.]

VIC. OK, Free, [have some beer why don't you]

FREE.	**RAM./MAGGIE.**
[What? I'm just curious.]	[OK... so what do you two call yourselves?]

FREE./MAGGIE. [Lovers]

RAM. Lovers?

MAGGIE. [Lovers]

(*beat*)

RAM./MAGGIE. [But lovers can apply to... lovers seems vague...so how do you make the distinction between lets say less committed and more committed couples...?]

FREE./MAGGIE. [We don't need to. We're lovers]

RAM./MAGGIE. [Life-long lovers?]

    (FREE *laughs.*)

    [What's funny?]

FREE./MAGGIE. [Hearing people]

    (*beat*)

RAM. [What is that sign you used? Lovers –]

MAGGIE. (*MAGGIE demonstrates.*) [Lovers]

RAM. So this is [love] and then...

MAGGIE. [It breaks down to love-person]

RAM. Love person?

MAGGIE. Sure, same with any other sort of person, Teacher, Dancer... verb plus person.

RAM./MAGGIE. [That's a bit clinical]

MAGGIE. [Accurate. You are what you do.]

RAM./MAGGIE. Sure. Right.

    (*beat*)

    [I'm sorry, I should track down my cousin, my flight leaves in a couple of hours]

VIC. Already?

RAM./MAGGIE. [It's been great Vic, really]

    (*RAM gives her a quick hug.*)

VIC./MAGGIE. [Definitely! Yeah, stay in touch, ok?]

RAM./MAGGIE. [Yes! Nice meeting you both!]

FREE. [Bye]

MAGGIE. [You too, a pleasure! *(to* FREE*)* [Behave!]

FREE. [What?]

    (*RAM exits.*)

VIC. Look at him go, oh oh, [watch watch watch]... he's going to check all his pockets right when he hits the door, side side chest back pockets, aaand – pat pat pat pat pat, mmmm – mmm – every fucking time!

FREE. [OK, Mom.]

VIC. [<u>Ok, Mom</u>]? [<u>What</u>]'s that supposed to mean? And what the hell is [<u>your problem</u>]? [<u>You</u>] just feel like being a [<u>bitch</u>]? This is why we don't hang out, [<u>you</u>] fucking go out of your way to [<u>embarrass me</u>]!

Fuck this – Hey Ram, wait up! I'll ride with you ok?

(VIC exits.)

You're getting the big sendoff, baby!

(Sound of kazoos, laughter, bar crowd gathers to see **RAM** *off.)*

*(***FREE*** *signs after* **VIC.***)*

(ASL on screen)

FREE. [Hey this was really great! Next time, don't call! I'd rather sit at home picking my nose!]

*(***MAGGIE*** *taps her.)*

[What?]

MAGGIE. [I'm not voicing that]

FREE. [Why the hell not?]

MAGGIE. [I'm not yelling at your sister in the middle of a bar]

FREE. [No?]

MAGGIE. [No]

FREE. [Wussy]

MAGGIE. [Bite me]

FREE. [Let's go home]

(Lights fade as **MAGGIE** *and* **FREE** *get up to leave bar. Kazoos, laughter, noise fade.)*

Scene Two

(Lights up on **FREE** *and* **MAGGIE**'s *apartment, they're just getting home, getting ready for bed, in mid-debate. Their home is quiet.)*

(This scene is in ASL only, English appears on screen.)

MAGGIE. [I wasn't speaking for you, I was talking about ASL]

FREE. [Well, next time let me talk about ASL]

MAGGIE. [I was just…ok fine]

FREE. [It's no big deal, I'm just mentioning it]

MAGGIE. [Ok, whatever, we'll never see him again, it doesn't matter]
[I didn't realize he was leaving town right away, I feel bad, we should have left so they could be alone to say goodbye…]

FREE. [He was not interested in being alone with my sister]

MAGGIE. [How do you know?]

FREE. [I know.]
[That poem he read is pointless]

MAGGIE. *(laughs)* [Yeah well, you think all poetry is pointless]

FREE. [You said it's trying to describe love, right?]

MAGGIE. [Right…]

FREE. [There's already a perfectly good description of love. Sex.]

*(**FREE** pulls **MAGGIE** close, they, kiss. **FREE** starts laughing.)*

FREE. [I think it's interesting that a hearing professor hates translations too]

MAGGIE. [He doesn't hate translations]

FREE. [He said, 'I hate translations'.]

MAGGIE. [He didn't mean it literally. He translates all day]

FREE. [Doesn't mean he likes it]

MAGGIE. [No, he lives in a state of misery, every time he opens his mouth]

FREE. [OK, you have no sense of humor about this]

MAGGIE. [You're not making a joke, you're picking a fight.]

FREE. [What fight? We live in an English world, we'll keep living in an English world, no one's threatening your language. Why can't you just admit that translation is not as good, and stop being so defensive –]

MAGGIE. [You're not saying translation is not as good, you're saying translation sucks]

FREE. [Same thing]

MAGGIE. [It is not the same thing, and no one is saying that translation is just as good, just that maybe it has its own value, and it's better than nothing]

FREE. (not on screen) [Blablabla]

MAGGIE. [What?]

FREE. [I've seen this speech before. "This has this kind of value, this has that kind of value," – nothing is absolutely like anything else, but that's ok, let's mix it all up and see what comes out.]

MAGGIE. [Whatever. Vic's right, you're in a mood.]

FREE. [Vic is the same as our mother.]

MAGGIE. [You don't give her a chance]

FREE. [I know exactly what happens – she falls in love every week, with someone impossible, she's fun, she's a party girl, she'll cry when he doesn't call, make a big tragedy out if it, she's known him one week and he's the love of her life, whatever, I'm

bored. Trust me, she's my sister, I know her a lot
better than you. Can we finish with this subject?]

MAGGIE. [You brought it up.]

FREE. [OK, well I'm done with it.]

MAGGIE. [Well I thought it was an interesting evening]

FREE. [Good for you]

MAGGIE. [It was fun to do something different, maybe
if you were willing to try –]

(FREE *turns lights out, conversation is cut off.*)

(*Silence.* MAGGIE*'s last words linger on screen.*
MAGGIE *turns light back on.*)

FREE. [What?]

MAGGIE. [I was talking]

FREE. [Sorry. I didn't see. What were you saying?]

(*beat*)

MAGGIE. [You're tired]

FREE. [That's what you were saying?]

MAGGIE. [No, that's what I'm saying now. Let's go to
bed.]

FREE. [Fine.]

(FREE *exits.* MAGGIE *turns out light as she exits.*)

Scene Three

(Night. **RAM** *is at his computer. He is back to his normal self, a private, lonely.)*

RAM. *(He proofs an Email out loud as it appears on screen.)*

TO: Birju@clubcacophony.com

FROM: Balaram

RE: Visit

Dear cousin,

Thanks for hosting my vacation, I had a great time. I'm back to work now, and as dull as I ever was. Your lifestyle is not for me in the long term, though I appreciate your efforts on my behalf.

My regards to all the staff and tell Vic thanks for a memorable week...

*(***RAM*** makes a face, deletes back to 'and'.)*

...and Vic. And stop telling my mother stories, or I'll tell your mother about your parties!

Cheers,

Ram

(He sends, thinks a moment, starts a new email out loud)

TO: MeenaJoshi@freenet.uk

FROM: Balaram

RE: Visit

Dear Mum, I'm back at work after an exhausting week of relaxing in Birju's company. Tell Auntie my lips are sealed, she will hear none of his secrets from me.

As for Birju's loose lips, no I did NOT meet anyone 'special' while I was there.

*(***RAM*** murmurs 'asshole'.)*

Professor Masson is beginning research for a new book of Sanskrit love poems translated into English. I am in charge of making the first selections.

Perhaps this summer I might take a week off to come visit.

I love you,

Ram

(He sends. Sits. Turns off light.)

(blackout)

(Beep. **VIC** *V.O. leaving a message, club noise in background.*

(words on screen)

VIC. Hey Ram.! It's Vic Jones here, miss you, so how's it going – ? You know, I think you left something at my apartment – I realized you don't have my number – give me a call, it's – uh – 555..., what?? No, I'm on the phone, asshole – ok ok! Sorry about that, it's nuts here, so anyway, my number is 555 —

(blackout)

Scene Four

(Lights up on **MAGGIE** & **FREE**'s *apartment.* **VIC** *has been drinking and is having trouble remembering to sign, so* **MAGGIE** *interprets.)*

(ASL not on screen)

VIC. [Fuck you!]

MAGGIE. Vic!

VIC. Vic shit Vic fuck you

MAGGIE. [Vic, I'm just saying that you need to calm down, it's impossible to have a conversation like this]

VIC./MAGGIE. Oh, I need to calm down? You know what, [you're a fucking snob! Magg Magg, Magna Cum Laude. Oh wait, let me show you my high school diploma, cuz I got an A in English, you hag!]

FREE. [Maggie. Go.]

MAGGIE. [I can stay]

VIC./MAGGIE. [Oh no, you go, who needs you? My sister and I communicated just fine before you, during you, and after you]

MAGGIE. [I'm staying, we're fine]

FREE. *(to* **VIC***)* [Hey! You sign like shit, and you know it. We never 'communicated' at all before Maggie.]

MAGGIE. [Free…]

VIC./MAGGIE. [I sign a fuckload better than you talk!] [Free the Deaf Dyke! That's what they call you at home, the Deaf Dyke!]

[I'm the only one that comes to see you two. And you never fucking support me! Not once]

MAGGIE. [(We support you)]

VIC./MAGGIE. *(cont.)* [It's not like he's too good for me! Is that what you think? You think he's too good for me? I should go back to like Jake the asshole?]

FREE. [Wait, wait, wait, you're back with Jake?]

VIC. [No, I'm not back with Jake!] I'm fucking moving on! Cuz you see this? [This is our poem! Ram read me this poem the first night we met, and it's a fucking love poem, ok?] What the hell do you know anyway –

FREE. [Stop! Ram is not interested in you. He's not calling you.]

VIC. [Oh, fuck you, so he hasn't called me, it's been, what, a week? He's busy!]

FREE. [Stop drinking]

(hurt silence)

VIC./MAGGIE. [So why do you get a Professor and I don't, huh? I graduated high school just like you. Better than you. Maggie, did you check her grades before you started fucking her? When she filled out the application...] *(starts laughing)* [for the damn job...check her transcript? Or maybe the competition wasn't so hot, you're getting older after all and ... whew... it can be tough at those singles mixers when you're interestingly – abled like the two of you...] [Deaf and Boring walk into a bar...]

(MAGGIE stops interpreting to interrupt her.)

MAGGIE. [Stop it. Why are you doing this?]

VIC. [I'm making myself feel better]

FREE. [Do you feel better?]

VIC./MAGGIE. [I do feel better, thank you Free.! I feel free! Free. to say whatever I want because, hell, no one listens to me anyway! Freeeee. Freeeeeee. Oh! Funny funny stuff.]

FREE. [Get out...]

(MAGGIE shakes her head at FREE to wait for VIC to calm down.)

(They have a quick exchange in ASL, English on screen.)

MAGGIE. [She can't drive]

FREE. [Then she can walk, and you can stop interpreting, I don't need to hear her]

MAGGIE. [She's just lashing out, she's hurt – you could have a little empathy here]

FREE. [Why? You're taking care of it.]

(screen off)

VIC. *(collapsing onto the couch)* I don't feel good

FREE. [If you're going to vomit, go to the bathroom]

VIC./MAGGIE. [Fucking men, I wish I was a dyke.] [God I feel like shit, I hate this.]

MAGGIE. [Stay put, I'll get you some water, should I make coffee?]

VIC./MAGGIE. [I fucking fucked up. I hate this! I hate me!]

FREE./MAGGIE. [What are you talking about?]

VIC./MAGGIE. [Stupid, stupid, I called him from the club and left this dumbass message – "no big deal – hey, I think you left something at my apartment – give me a call…" like a fucking loser…]

FREE./MAGGIE. [Did he leave something at your apartment?]

VIC./MAGGIE. [No. I mean, what am I, twelve? I'm just so tired of this shit, you know? I don't like being alone]

FREE. [Look at me! Maybe you need to be alone]

VIC./MAGGIE. [I hate my life. What if I never like my life?]

FREE. [You'll like it better without some asshole hanging around making you miserable]

VIC./MAGGIE. Shit shit shit – Magg, [I want to call him] again, ok? [Come on], before I lose my nerve, and I want to sound like I'm not a complete asshole –

FREE. [He doesn't want to talk to you!]

VIC./MAGGIE. [Fine, whatever, he doesn't have to call back, right? I just need to call him.]

FREE. [So fuck him. He's a loser]

VIC./MAGGIE. [He's not a loser, he's just a nice guy! What, I don't deserve that?]
[Yeah. Just butt out. I want to call him. Maggie, I want to call him!]

MAGGIE. [OK. OK. Let's just, hang on – let's get some paper] –

(**FREE** *is being ignored.*)

FREE. [You don't need me for this, I'm taking a shower]

MAGGIE. [All I can advise is honesty. I mean, is that what you want to hear?]

VIC. OK

MAGGIE. OK?

VIC. I mean, OK, whatever the fuck you say. Really. Sorry about mouthing off earlier, I was just... you know. [Sorry.]

MAGGIE. [Vic, we love you, you know that. But he doesn't sound like he's...]
[But that's ok! You can call him, and then you'll have tried.]
[First things first – you should write it down, so you don't stumble, I do that with important phone calls. Here.]
[Ok, so tell me how you feel!]

(**FREE** *exits, frustrated.*)

VIC. Nice shrink-voice

MAGGIE. [Vic]

VIC. OK, OK, I feel... I want him to come back.

MAGGIE. [You want him to come back, and...?]

(**MAGGIE** *notices that* **FREE** *has left.*)

[Come on.]

VIC. And sweep me off my feet, shit!
   He's nice… and he thinks I'm just this… I don't know what, and that pisses me off –

MAGGIE. [OK. OK, let's keep it simple –]

   (Beep. crossfade to **RAM** *listening to Vic's voice mail.)*

   (words on screen)

VIC. *(V.O.)* Hi Ram! I wasn't totally honest earlier, you didn't leave anything at my apartment except me. I miss you, and I'd like to keep talking to you. I hope you call me. Maybe I'll shoot you an email, and then you'll have my address, if you want it. Ok? Bye.

   *(***RAM*** deletes the message.* "MESSAGE DELETED.*")*

   (He sits at his computer working.)

   (Lights come up slowly on Maggie and Free's apartment. **MAGGIE** *has gone to bed,* **VIC** *is passed out on the couch.)*

   *(***FREE*** can't sleep, she covers* **VIC** *with a blanket, looks at her for a moment.)*

   (She finds the poem on the floor and starts to tuck it under **VIC***'s hand, then stops and reads it. As she reads, the English translation of Ram's poem from top of play appears on the screen.)*

   *(***FREE*** signs to herself, making sense of it.)*

   (ASL not on screen)

FREE. [Foolish man – Foolish people… value things, not important, holding on to worthless things is not safe… freedom…what is freedom? Emotion should be valued.]
   [My opinion – naked… love, sex… her dress off… eye contact… I fall… emotions soar –]

(She reads the poem again. She strokes **VIC** *'s forehead.)*

(ASL ON SCREEN)

[Beautiful sister. He's a coward.]

*(***VIC*** *sleeps.)*

(Suddenly angry with Ram, **FREE** *grabs her Blackberry and enters his email address off the letterhead.)*

(email appears on screen)

TO: balaram@bostonuniversity.edu
FROM: jonesgirl@peoplelinc.com
RE: YOUR POEM

fool
you do not value emotion
you are not free
woman dancing, eyes connect, naked body, heart
soars –
this is free

*(***FREE*** *sends, feels a little better.)*

(She tucks the poem under **VIC** *'s hand.)*

(Sits and thinks. Lonely.)

*(***RAM*** *sees Free's email.)*

RAM. Oh, shit…

(Her email affects him, he types.)

TO: jonesgirl
FROM: Balaram
RE: Re. YOUR POEM

You're right. I'm a coward.
I'm not good at relationships with real people, and
I've behaved badly. I have always lacked romantic
courage. Except possibly on paper.
Sorry.
Ram.

(Free's Blackberry lights up. **FREE** *reads, surprised. She feels guilty, types.)*

TO: Balaram
FROM: Jonesgirl

I am sorry. I am rude. your life, your choice.
I like your poem. it describes love well

*(***RAM*** *types.)*

TO: Jonesgirl
FROM: Balaram

I like your version. Very to the point as translations go.

*(***FREE*** *smiles, types.)*

TO: Balaram
FROM: Jonesgirl

translation sucks, remember?
I like mind meld like star trek for communication
:)

*(***RAM*** *smiles. Types.)*

TO: Jonesgirl
FROM: Balaram

That would simplify things

(lights fade)

(blackout)

PART II

Scene One

(V.O. **RAM** *reciting Bhavabhuti's* Uttararamacar-
ita, *I. 27. Sanskrit on screen. Simultaneously* **FREE**
*in lone spotlight/streetlight performs the poem in
ASL.)*

RAM.

Kimapi kimapi mandam mandam asaktiyogad

Aviralitakapolam jalpator akramena

Asithilaparirambhavyaprtaikadosnor

Aviditagatayama ratrir eva vyaramsit

(Lights up on **FREE** *receiving an email on her
Blackberry, stopping to read it. The email appears
on screen.)*

TO: Jonesgirl
FROM: Balaram

Jonesgirl! I gave a talk on this poem this morning,
see what you think –)

(Lights up on **RAM** *speaking to students positioned
in the audience. He is not a naturally charismatic
speaker, but does his best to engage. The result is
awkward and he laughs at too many of his own
jokes.)*

                              (Email cont.)

Deep in love	Deep in love
Cheek leaning on cheek	Cheek leaning on cheek
we talked	we talked

Of whatever came into
our minds
Just as it came
Slowly oh
Slowly
With our arms twined
Tightly around us
And the hours passed
and we
Did not know it
Still talking when
The night had gone

Not bad, eh? Now, as the
story goes the
poet Bhavabhuti
brought the Uttara –
macarita to the great
Kalidasa,
interrupting him in the
middle of a chess
game. Not just this piece
that I just read
you, understand, but the
whole
Uttaramacarita! You'll
have to take my
word for it, it's not a
quick read. He
interrupts Kalidasa in his
chess match to
recite him this great new
work, and recites
it from beginning to end
with not one
interruption from the
great master!

Of whatever came into
our minds
Just as it came
Slowly oh
Slowly
With our arms twined
Tightly around us
And the hours passed
and we
Did not know it
Still talking when
The night had gone

Not bad, right? I follow
up with this
anecdote, it's very funny.
The poet
Bhavabhuti brought the
Uttaramacarita to
the great Kalidasa, interrupting him in the
middle of a chess game.

Not just this piece but
the whole
Uttaramacarita –

it's not a quick read!

He interrupts Kalidasa in
his chess match to
recite this great new
work, and recites it
from beginning to end
with not one
interruption from the
great master!

Unlike today, in those
days all things
would stop for great art.
No warning or
preparation, but Kalidas
stops his playing
instantly to listen. These
days we stop for
commercials, not for art,
eh? Hahah!
Art does not flow unin-
terrupted these
days... does it?
Does it? No!
And there you
have another reason to
study Sanskrit!

But to return to my pri-
mary point in this
possibly apocryphal
story. When he
finished, Kalidasa leaned
forward! He
moved one piece on the
board, check –
mating his opponent.
And then he
turned to Bhavabhuti
and said,
"There is but one imper-
fection in your entire
poem. There is one
letter 'm' too many!

Unlike today, in those
days all things
would stop for great art.
No warning or
preparation, but Kali-
dasa stops his playing
instantly to listen! These
days we stop for
commercials, not for art.

Art does not flow unin-
terrupted these days!

See I thought that was
funny, but no one
laughed.

Anyway, when he fin-
ished,
Kalidasa leaned forward.

He moved one piece on
the board,
check – mating his
opponent.
And then he turned to
Bhavabhuti
and said,

"There is but one imper-
fection in your entire
poem. There is one
letter 'm' too many!

*(Sanskrit returns to screen briefly before email con-
tinues.)*

You see this word?
'Eva'…? It was
originally 'Evam' mean-
ing in effect that
the lovers spoke and
spoke until the night
had passed! But with the
removal of this
one letter – 'm' – the
word became 'eva'…
'Aviditagatayama ratrir
eva vyaramsit'…
and now the lovers
spoke and spoke and
although night passed
they continued to speak.
For how long? Perhaps
for all eternity? With the
removal of one 'm'!
One 'm'. This is San-
skrit! So! If you find
this fascinating, if you
find this
'm' here or there fasci-
nating – you should
definitely study Sanskrit!
And if not, hang on to
this photocopy
and impress a girl on
your next date! Or
a boy! It works just as
well for the ladies,
enjoy it as my gift. I can
take any
questions now?

Look at the poem again
– you see the word
'Eva'? It was originally
'Evam' which
means that the lovers
spoke until the night
had passed! But take
away that
 'm' and the word
becomes 'eva'

And now the lovers
spoke and spoke and
although night passed
they continued to speak.
For how long? Per-
haps forever? With the
removal of one 'm'!
One 'm'. This is San-
skrit!
I find this fascinating!

I find this 'm' here or
there fascinating!
I don't know if they did.
But I told them to keep
the photocopy
and impress their next
date!

What do you think?

R.

(screen switches to IM.)

No questions?	Hello?
You're sure?	Did I put you to sleep?
Well, that's alright, enjoy the rest of	
your sampler week and I hope to see	Half of them were asleep.
some of you next semester.	
Oh, yes sorry, you in the back?	
Yes the cafeteria is across the plaza.	The other half were apparently starved
No problem.	and desperate to find the cafeteria.

(Lights shift, **RAM** *is home, it's evening. The emails flash up on the screen as they are received, fading to black before the next one arrives.)*

TO: jonesgirl
FROM: BALARAM
Hello?
TO: Balaram
FROM: jonesgirl

I'm here.
good story. but truth is talk stops in morning.
poet was right.

TO: jonesgirl
FROM: balaram

It's an ideal, a beautiful ideal. Why do you think talk stops? Don't you think some people keep talking their whole lives?

TO: balaram
FROM: jonesgirl

not really. life goes on in morning, people get out of bed and have to go. that is the problem. then you are apart all day and when you come home you are different person.

TO: jonesgirl
FROM: balaram

Cynic

TO: balaram
FROM: jonesgirl

math
work, sleep, eat. time together is very little.

TO: jonesgirl
FROM: balaram

That's a sad thought. What about us?

TO: balaram
FROM: jonesgirl

talk at night. apart in day. everything is different.

TO: jonesgirl
FROM: balaram

I'll call you tomorrow morning.

(Lights fade up on **FREE**. *She is confused and doesn't respond.)*

Vic?

(FREE *drops the Blackberry and backs away from it. How the hell did this happen?)*

Are you there?

(FREE *can't decide whether to respond or cease communication. Finally she types –)*

TO: balaram
FROM: jonesgirl

why?

(*FREE waits.*)

TO: jonesgirl
FROM: balaram

So we can talk.
Cheek to cheek

(*Screen goes dark. Lights fade completely on* **RAM**.)

(*The door opens and* **MAGGIE** *comes in. She's late.*)

(**FREE** *conceals her Blackberry, turns her frustration on* **MAGGIE**.)

(*ASL on screen*)

FREE. [Where the fuck were you?]

MAGGIE. [We got to talking, what are you doing up?]

FREE. [Waiting for you, what do you think?]

MAGGIE. [I'm sorry, I thought you'd be asleep]

>   (*Beat.* **FREE** *stares at her Blackberry, then puts it away.*)
>
>   [Hey, what's wrong?]

FREE. [Whatever, I don't care, I need to get some sleep]

MAGGIE. [It was a really good party, you should have been there! Everyone asked about you]

FREE. [No reason for me to go be bored]

MAGGIE. [I think you'd like some of the faculty if you got to know them.]

FREE. [It's not like you ever come out with my friends]

MAGGIE. [Twice, I couldn't make it. Twice!]

FREE. [But you're so important, you have to go to a party every weekend]

MAGGIE. [You should get out of the house, see more people – maybe then you wouldn't be so crabby all the time]

FREE. [Don't try to psychoanalyze me. I'm crabby because you stayed out until 2 am. I'm crabby because I worried about you. I'm crabby because now I haven't slept and I have work in the morning, that's why I'm crabby]

MAGGIE. [OK, you're pissed, I'm sorry]

FREE. [Good night.]

(FREE *exits. Blackout.*)

Scene Two

(Telephone rings. Lights up on VIC *just waking up, answering her phone. [words on screen]*

VIC. H'lo?

(Lights up on RAM.*)*

RAM. Good morning jones-girl

VIC. Hello? Oh shit, I'm late! Who is this?

RAM. It's Ram.

VIC. ...Ram?? Oh, hey! Hey you! Oh, wow.

RAM. I'm sorry, you're in a rush.

VIC. No, no, what's going on? I'm just, I made a stupid morning hair appointment, but I probably would have missed it anyway, so whatever, right? How are you?

RAM. I'm fine, I'm just getting ready for class.
Listen, you go to your appointment, I can call again later.

VIC. Oh, no, no, it's not a big deal.

RAM. I have to get ready anyway, same time tomorrow better?

VIC. Yeah? Yeah!

RAM. Have a good day?

VIC. Ok. Bye.

*(*RAM *hangs up.)*

*(*VIC *is numb for a moment, then does a wild dance.)*

YES! YESYESYESYESYEEEESSS!!

(Crossfade to MAGGIE *and* FREE*'s bedroom that evening.)*

MAGGIE. Yes! Get sleep! Go to sleep! Ok, good night.

*(*MAGGIE *hangs up the phone, goes back to correcting papers.)*

(Scene in ASL only, English on screen)

FREE. [Vic again?]

MAGGIE. [She can't sleep. 'Will he call, what if he
doesn't call, do I call him, was I supposed to
call him, no he said he'd call me…!??' She's so
excited.]

(Long beat. MAGGIE works, FREE mulls.)

FREE. [Do you remember when we first met? We used
to talk all the time, I mean non – stop!]
[I loved our hands. I loved the way they moved
together. Sexy.]

MAGGIE. [Yeah]

FREE. [That night under the streetlight?]

MAGGIE. [Our streetlight.]

(Streetlight begins to glow.)

FREE. [It was too dark to talk, so finally you just stopped
under the streetlight and we were signing, and we
just stood there talking and talking trying to finish
our conversation, but it never ended, until finally
it started snowing and we were too cold to stand
there any longer.]

MAGGIE. [And then we ran all the way home]

FREE. [Adrenaline!]

(MAGGIE laughs.)

[I miss that]

MAGGIE. Mm! [But also, I loved the way you said things!
Maybe I just love Sign. I love the directness…
and then it's suddenly so beautiful and poetic
that you want to cry because you're not stuck to
words, you're just speaking in pure meaning – like
poetry. Any image or connection or rhythm works,
so long as the truth is told. It's so succinct, and yet
so –]

FREE. *(gets in bed)* [Move over]

MAGGIE. [...Isn't it an amazing thing, I thought, to walk around in daily life and have your first language be poetry, and not prose! To speak poetry wherever you go! It's like being Shakespeare!]

FREE. [Not really. Being Deaf is not like being Shakespeare.]

(FREE *picks up a magazine. Streetlight fades.*)

MAGGIE. [Hey. I thought we were talking]

FREE. [We were. I've heard this story before, you tell it all the time.]

MAGGIE. [Because we're talking about when we met.] [So it's an old story, were you going to tell me something amazing that I've never heard before about when we first met?]

FREE. [No.]

MAGGIE. [Fine. Then why are you attacking me?]

FREE. [I'm not attacking, I'm just not very interested in hearing you say the exact same things that you always say to every person we meet.]

MAGGIE. [That happens to be a good memory for me, that's why I tell people that story. And you don't need to try to ruin it for me, just because you're in a mood. You're always in a mood these days.] [That was a revelation for me. Meeting you was a revelation. The sign we used in my family for my sister was stilted and clumsy and the signing world you showed me was –]

FREE. [I know all this. I've heard it before. It's great.]

MAGGIE. [Oh, ok, screw off.]

(beat)

FREE. [I want you to stop encouraging Vic with this Ram guy. You know he's not really interested in her.]

MAGGIE. [So then why did he call her this morning?]

FREE. [Who knows what he wants.]

MAGGIE. [Maybe a girlfriend?]

FREE. [He's just being polite or something. He'll get
bored and stop calling her, and she'll move on to
the next guy]

MAGGIE. [Why won't you let her grow?]

FREE. [This guy doesn't want her! This is how you want
to teach her self – respect? By helping her chase
some guy around?]

MAGGIE. [Everyone should be allowed to change, to
create themselves.]

FREE. [...by teaching her to be like you?]

MAGGIE. [Oh please, I helped her leave a voicemail, I
listened.]
[Even if he doesn't last, what she's doing is power-
ful, she's taking charge of her own life]

FREE. [And you're God]

MAGGIE. (MAGGIE *starts speaking as she signs, upset.*)
[And I'm what??]

FREE. [You're molding her to be like you. But she's
not one of your students paying you to make them
more like you.]

MAGGIE. [Who do I mold to be like me? Who? Are you
serious? Do you seriously think that? About me? I
want to mold people?]

FREE. [You're talking.]

MAGGIE. [What??]

FREE. [You're talking. When you get upset, you speak.
English. Your signing goes to hell. You can't speak
2 languages at once. You know that.]

(silence)

*(FREE receives an IM, leaves the bedroom to check
her Blackberry. IM on screen.)*

TO: jonesgirl
FROM: balaram

It was nice hearing your voice this morning. Sorry I woke you up.

Vic?

(FREE hesitates, glances back at MAGGIE who turns off light and goes to bed.)

FREE. [Shit. Shit shit shit shit shit shit shit!]

(Finally FREE types back.)

TO: balaram
FROM: jonesgirl

I can't sleep
TO: jonesgirl
FROM: balaram

Me neither. Why can't you sleep?

TO: balaram
FROM: jonesgirl

too many words in my head, shoving, moving everything around

(FREE sits on couch with Blackberry close for comfort.)

(Lights slowly fade leaving only screen.)

TO: jonesgirl
FROM: balaram

What words?

(blackout)

TO: balaram
FROM: jonesgirl

like bumps on a road, tripping, bumping, can't relax.
you?

(blackout)

TO: jonesgirl
FROM: balaram

Words that rhyme, I get in a rut: old, fold, cold, sold, mold, told, drives me crazy. Blablablabla. Solitaire helps. That usually flushes the words out.

(blackout)

TO: balaram
FROM: jonesgirl

funny, I'll try it
good night

(blackout)

TO: jonesgirl
FROM: balaram

Good night

(blackout)

Scene Three

(Lights up on VIC and MAGGIE in the apartment. MAGGIE is searching for a book. FREE enters.)

(ASL not on screen)

MAGGIE. [There's this one poem I've loved since I was like twelve. It's called 'When You Are Old']. – Aha! got it!

VIC. You were reading poetry when you were 12? OK, I'm screwed!

(VIC sees FREE.)

Free, [I'm screwed]! Maggie's been [reading poetry since she was 12], I'll never catch up!

MAGGIE. [Hey sweetie!]   **FREE.**
[Hi]

[Oh no, this particular
poem was on a *Twilight
Zone* episode, and I was
hooked on the *Twilight
Zone*! So my dad gave me
this book of poetry so I
wouldn't just watch TV
all day, and I'd have
some form of literary
enlightenment. I wasn't
that much of a nerd!

I think back then I was
reading Nancy Drew.]
[– What's up?]

VIC. [I read] Nancy Drew!

MAGGIE. [Yeah?]

VIC. [Yeah!]
Aaah! I liiiiiiike poetry!!!! I do! I [loooove poetry]!!!

MAGGIE. [Yes! A convert! So what's Ram working on
now?]

VIC. Ok, [I feel stupid], [we don't have to talk about
my shit,] I'm just – [he calls me]. Like [every
morning] almost, it's – I don't know. [I'll shut up],
you talk more. I'm going crazy, it's like I can't shut
up about it – AAAAH!

MAGGIE. [This is so exciting!]

VIC. Ok, I [want to see your poem]!

MAGGIE. [OK, my poem –]

VIC. [Gimme gimme]! I need to [read some more
poetry], you know? Familiarize myself with the
'Genr'ah!" [Right Free?]

FREE. [Surc]

MAGGIE. [You know, that's the amazing thing about poetry, to me. It's immortal, it speaks directly to the soul, words keep resonating, I read them, you read them, it connects us to the past to the future. Free doesn't always understand my passion for the written word…]

FREE. [Nope]

MAGGIE. [It's not her thing. Here it is – It's the one about growing old, you know it Free. –]

FREE. [I need to change]

*(**FREE** exits abruptly. **MAGGIE** is hurt.)*

(beat)

VIC. Sorry.

MAGGIE. What? Oh! No, it's [not you], we're having some sort of… things are a bit off lately. Free [doesn't like] [poetry]. [Which is my job], so bummer, right?
Here, why don't you read it, maybe I'll start some tea or something…

*(Beat. **VIC** abruptly changes the subject.)*

VIC. Hey, did Free ever tell you how she saved my life?

MAGGIE. What?

*(**FREE** re-enters, **VIC** catches her attention.)*

VIC. Hey Free, [remember Mom's hike]?

FREE. [What?]

MAGGIE. [Are you tired?]

*(**FREE** shrugs.)*

VIC. No seriously, [Mom's] fucking [hike, remember?]

FREE. [Mom didn't hike]

VIC. When we [lived near] that [campground]

*(**FREE** is blank, then it dawns on her.)*

FREE./VIC. [Oh right, the campground by the freeway]

VIC. Right! And there was all this undeveloped [land behind it]! So, Magg, Mom decides a fucking [wilderness walk] would be a [good idea], right? And [she wakes us all up] at some [dark-ass] hour. None of us have ever hiked before!

FREE. [I remember…]

VIC. And [Mom's all worried about Free. –] What if we lose Free! She had some crazy system so that someone [can always see Free], like she has to always [walk in the middle] –

FREE./VIC. [That's right, we're walking in a line, and someone yells – 'Free's here!]' like every few minutes!

MAGGIE. [Funny!]

FREE. [I can't believe you remember this.]

VIC. The place [is so flat that we can't lose Free] if we try, We can [see the –]

FREE./VIC. [Holiday Inn across the freeway]!

MAGGIE. [I love your mom…]

VIC. Oh no no, [wait], that's not the good part! [I'm walking] along, and suddenly [Free shoves] me down, and [grabs this snake] out of nowhere by like the neck, and [throws it] off into the bushes!

FREE. [That's right!]

VIC. [So I start screaming]

FREE. [You were like AAAAH]

VIC. The [boys are screaming! Mom's screaming! Free's completely silent]. We're all [running] to get back through the campground and the fuck out of there!

FREE. [We woke up everyone in the campground]

VIC. [Mom's yelling] 'Frida! Frida! Did it [bite you]? Did it [bite you]?' We get to the camp office, and they've got this [chart on the wall]

FREE./VIC. [Snake chart, from the department of wildlife or something]

VIC. [Free identifies the snake], and sure enough it's [poisonous]!

MAGGIE. [Oh my god, then what?]

VIC. [Emergency room]! Three towns away, all of us in the [old white van,] fucking nighmare, [mom's crying]the whole way!

FREE. [I was fine]

VIC. Yeah, [Free] was [fine], not a mark on her, [totally chill, snake handling? Whatever!]

MAGGIE. [Wow! *(to* FREE*)* How come you never told me that story?]

FREE. [It was no big deal. If it hadn't been poisonous, I would have snuck it in her backpack, scared the crap out of her]

VIC. [Bitch! Wait, you knew it was poisonous? Before we went out that day]

FREE. [Rattlesnake, sure, there was a chart in the camping office]

MAGGIE. [Free notices things like charts in camping offices.]

VIC. [Holy shit, you saved my life! Big, brave, big sister!! You've always got my back!]

FREE. [Yeah yeah yeah, you're welcome]

VIC. OK, that's it! I should [go!] You guys need your [alone time,] and [I need]my beauty [sleep]so I can be fresh when [Ram calls in the morning!] So we can [talk, and talk, and talk]

(FREE is getting tense again.)

MAGGIE. [Do you ever call him]

VIC. [No. I like that he calls me.]It's nice, you know I think that was [the problem] at first was [me calling him, he's an old fashioned kind of guy]

FREE. [Don't get too attached.]

(beat)

VIC. What?

MAGGIE. [Free! Why shouldn't she get attached?]

FREE. [It's not real, it's just talk. Just don't get attached,
I don't want you to get hurt again.]

VIC. [You don't want to see me hurt?]

Oh…ok.

Then you should [shut up] then, shouldn't you?

(silence)

MAGGIE. Vic…

(VIC gathers her things and leaves.)

(ASL on screen)

MAGGIE. [That wasn't nice]

FREE. [It's true, she's got a shitty track record]

(silence)

MAGGIE. [Do you want to go camping this weekend?]

FREE. [No, I need to figure some stuff out.]

MAGGIE. [Fine]

(FREE needs to get it off her chest.)

FREE. [It's stupid, I sent this guy this email, and he got
confused and thinks I'm someone else, and now I
have to fix the confusion, it's a mess. Busy weekend.]

MAGGIE. [Fine]

(blackout)

Scene Four

(Lights up on **RAM** *typing. Words appear on screen.)*

TO: jonesgirl
FROM: balaram

I had a strange dream

*(***RAM*** gets a glass of milk, waits, nothing. He gets a newspaper, stops, checks, nothing. Waits.)*

(Lights up on **FREE**. *She doesn't want to write back, but can't think of a way out. Finally she types:)*

TO: balaram
FROM: jonesgirl

hi

*(***RAM*** perks up.)*

TO: jonesgirl
FROM: balaram

Hi there. I was getting worried.
It was the strangest thing, everything that happened in my dream, I was typing it. Every word, every gesture. It was fun at first, but then suddenly it became hard to keep up. The letters were shifting on the keys, there was this clackety-clacking like those old typewriters rushing me, I started to panic, hyperventilate... I woke up in a cold sweat. What do you think of that?

(screen black)

Do you write to me in your dreams?

TO: balaram
FROM: jonesgirl

no

(She tries to hold back, but can't resist getting drawn in.)

I dream about my hands

TO: jonesgirl
FROM: balaram

Explain

TO: balaram
FROM: jonesgirl

lift your hands from the keyboard

TO: jonesgirl
FROM: balaram

OK

TO: balaram
FROM: jonesgirl

stop typing
lift them up. only pretend typing in the air. look
at your hands. hands like snow. like silent music.
you see it?

*(For a moment both their hands are signing snow
music. Piano emerges, then fades. After a moment
FREE types.)*

now there is no rush

*(**RAM** is moved, he starts to type something, but hesitates.)*

*(**FREE** shakes off the moment, makes her decision,
types.)*

I've decided we should stop.
we need to see real people.

*(**RAM** types.)*

TO: jonesgirl
FROM: balaram

We are real.

*(**FREE** types.)*

TO: balaram
FROM: jonesgirl

this is not real. just words.
like your poems. they talk, but they are not real.
time to move on

(RAM types.)

TO: jonesgirl
FROM: balaram

For me, words are real.
This is real.

(Beat. FREE is torn.)

Vic?

(FREE pulls herself together to end it, types.)

TO: balaram
FROM: jonesgirl

not for me

(blackout)

(– optional intermission –)

PART III

Scene One

(From 15th century anthology compiled by Kash-mirian Srivara. On screen in Sanskrit.)

(FREE in lone spotlight/streetlight recites in ASL)

RAM. *(V.O.)*
>Jaye dharitryah puram eva saram
>Pure grham sadmani caikadesah
>Tatrapi sayya sayane varastri
>Ratnojjvala rajyasukhasya saram

(Lights up. VIC and MAGGIE are on the phone, MAGGIE signs the conversation to FREE, RAM waits for VIC in bed.)

VIC. [He came to read me a poem]

MAGGIE. *(to FREE)* [He flew all the way here to read her a poem.]

>*(to VIC)* [I'm sure that's it, call me later]

VIC./MAGGIE. [Ok. Love you.]

MAGGIE. [I'm so happy for her!]

FREE. [I'm going to bed]

MAGGIE. [They remind me of us! Let's be romantic, let's talk all night, get stupid and exhausted –]

FREE. [Not tonight, ok?]

>*(FREE exits.)*

>*(The following scene between VIC and RAM may be made accessible using the screen, or may be interpreted into ASL by MAGGIE. If you choose ASL*

*access, the italicized stage directions apply. If not,
disregard them.)*

*(Frustrated, **MAGGIE** grabs her coat and heads
out. She arrives under the streetlight during **RAM** 's
poem.)**

*(**VIC** joins **RAM** in bed as he reads from a piece of
paper. The poem is on screen in English translation)*

RAM.

Conquering the whole earth

As I have done

The essence of it is one

City

In that city one house

In that house only one

Room

And even there one bed

In that bed the woman above all others

The essence of the kingdom's happiness

Shining like a jewel

*(Standing in the streetlight, **MAGGIE** interprets the
following scene into ASL.)**

VIC. Mmm.

RAM. Professor Masson is working with this poet, Bill
Merwin – it's good isn't it? I'm involved in the
actual translating now, can you believe it? So Bill,
the poet, brought me this piece at the office. He
was picking something up, and just stopped to
talk, just stopped. I don't know him well, but he
knows I'm on the project, so he asked my opinion.
So I read it right there on the spot. Twice.

VIC. I still can't believe you're here...

RAM. I can't either. I never thought of myself as spon-
taneous.

*Optional stage direction

VIC. Surprise!

So what did you say? About the poem?

RAM. I said 'Pardon me, Bill, but I must catch a plane!'

VIC. You did not!

RAM. No. I said 'it's fantastic.'

And then I told him I must catch a plane, and I came here to you.

I read it and I knew I had to come.

Listen, this is real. We are real.

VIC. I know.

RAM. It was as though he walked into my office and answered a question that I had been asking without even knowing I was asking it. He's such a sweet old gentleman, he didn't even wonder where I was rushing off to, just told me to keep this in case I thought of any suggestions for him. Suggestions! I don't imagine I could tell him anything, he's a poet!

VIC. But you're the Sanskrit expert.

RAM. That's why he asked me, of course.

But I really feel that he captured something here. Maybe not the exact thing, but something that I at least find beautiful. Surprisingly beautiful.

VIC. And you're pretty choosy.

RAM. I can't say of course if anyone else would care for it. A person who doesn't know the original poem, may have no interest. That's the fear isn't it, you translate something and what if people read it and think, oh, how dull Sanskrit poetry is, how silly, how overdone. And then all you have accomplished is to condemn it to further obscurity for fools like me to labor over. Alone.

VIC. I like it.

RAM. Yes?

VIC. I love it.

RAM. I'm glad. But then you're Vic. You're unique.
>   *(Lights fade on* **VIC** *and* **RAM.***)*
>   *(Streetlight fades on* **MAGGIE.***)**

*Optional stage direction

Scene 2

(screen only in blackout)

TO: jonesgirl
FROM: balaram

Good evening

(Lights fade up gradually. **MAGGIE** *is reading a book and* **RAM** *is waiting at his computer.* **FREE** *reads her Blackberry screen. Clearly it's not over between* **RAM** *and her/***VIC** *as she had hoped. She wants to kick something, instead she punches 2 keys, sends.)*

TO: balaram
FROM: jonesgirl

hi

*(***RAM** *pauses.)*

TO: jonesgirl
FROM: balaram

I want to kiss everyone I see, is that normal?

*(***FREE** *punches 2 more keys.)*

TO: balaram
FROM: jonesgirl

no

(Beat. **RAM** *is at a loss.)*

TO: jonesgirl
FROM: balaram

Say something

TO: balaram
FROM: jonesgirl

don't know what

TO: jonesgirl
FROM: balaram

Are you tired?

(He tries to draw her in.)

What's your favorite breakfast?

*(**FREE** pretends to be **VIC**, isn't happy about it.)*

TO: balaram
FROM: jonesgirl

gin

TO: jonesgirl
FROM: balaram

Favorite piece of clothing?

TO: balaram
FROM: jonesgirl

tall black boots

TO: jonesgirl
FROM: balaram

Most romantic thing?

*(**FREE** looks at **MAGGIE**, slips into truth.)*

TO: balaram
FROM: jonesgirl

streetlight

(Ram's truth)

TO: jonesgirl
FROM: balaram

A computer screen

*(Beat. **FREE** needs to get out.)*

TO: balaram
FROM: jonesgirl

I should go to bed

TO: jonesgirl
FROM: balaram

OK. Something is wrong.

TO: balaram
FROM: jonesgirl

no. I'm tired. good night

TO: jonesgirl
FROM: balaram

Good night

(Screen black. **FREE** *looks at* **MAGGIE**. **MAGGIE** *glances up.)*

(ASL on screen)

MAGGIE. [What?]

FREE. [Nothing. I love you.]

*(***MAGGIE*** *smiles.)*

(Sound of a telephone, lights shift to Vic's apartment, **VIC** *picks up the phone. Lights up on* **RAM***, looking a little panicked.)*

(words on screen)

RAM. Are you ok?

VIC. *(laughs)* Of course I am!

RAM. Yeah? Alright. I was worried about you.

VIC. Silly! You sound tired, what's up?

RAM. Vic, I need your word on something. Don't let me scare you away.

VIC. Don't flatter yourself, baby, I don't scare easy.

RAM. I mean it. Don't let me scare you away. If I'm saying all the wrong things, stop me. Tell me how to say it right, but don't change your mind about me. This is so important. If I weren't so awkward… This is so important to me. I've never felt this way about anyone else – and –

VIC. You're nervous too. Oh, thank fucking god, you're nervous too! I thought it was just me!

RAM. Are you joking? You're killing me!

VIC. Well, it's mutual.

RAM. Well, good.

VIC. Good.

RAM. So we'll be nervous together? Deal?

VIC. Hell yeah!

RAM. OK! I'll see you this weekend.

VIC. Seriously? What do they pay you Sanskrit professors?

RAM. Not enough, I'm going broke. Oh, talking is good. I miss you.

VIC. You could just move here.

RAM. Don't tempt me.

I wait for you at night. I wait for you to be sleepless too, to answer me, I can't sleep until after we talk. That's our true selves, isn't it. Our true secret selves.

(Beat. **VIC** *processes.)*

VIC. (*not on screen*) Mmm

RAM. (*cont.*) And I need rest, I need to sleep! God midterms are next week! Have you any idea?

I need to be there with you. In the same room as you. Not a computer screen away…

VIC. (*not on screen*) Yeah…

(lights fade)

(blackout)

Scene Three

(Banging in the dark. Lights up on **FREE** *and* **MAGGIE***'s apartment,* **VIC** *bursts in.)*

VIC. What the fuck, Maggie? I trusted you!

MAGGIE. Vic?

FREE. [Oh great, is she drunk again?]

VIC. [No! No! Look at me, Free!! Both of you, look at me very closely. I am not drunk. I am very very angry.]

MAGGIE. [Ok. About?]

VIC. [Ram called tonight]

MAGGIE. [That's great!]

VIC. [Yeah, great. It's great, you're great we're all great!] I'm not getting into it with you right now, so all I have to say to you is [don't you ever Fucking email him again!]

MAGGIE. [Ok. What?]

VIC. What? What? Oh, huh, what????
See I thought we were friends, [I told you] fucking [everything], and I thought you maybe didn't [think I'm a complete asshole], I actually am that [stupid]. But going behind my back... [That's fucking low. And really could have screwed shit up.]
[So don't call, don't email, whatever.]

MAGGIE. [What are you talking about?]

FREE. [You should go.]

VIC. Oh, that's [great, Free, always blame me, right? Princess Perfect can't do anything wrong!] You know she went [behind your back too. Have you been getting laid lately? Because Ram sure has.] *(to* **MAGGIE***)* Except [that he thought it was me!] That's who he was picturing*!* And I'm sorry, but [flesh and blood trumps nightime chitchat] any fucking day of the week!

MAGGIE. [Someone's been emailing Ram?]

VIC. [You! How many nights now? Huh?] You know, who gives a shit.

MAGGIE. [I didn't.]

VIC. Oh, shut the fuck up...!

FREE. [Sorry.]

(They glance at her.)

MAGGIE. [You're sorry about what, sweetie?]

FREE. [Sorry, my screw up. I fucked up.]

MAGGIE. [With what?]

(Beat. **VIC** *realizes.)*

VIC. Oh no no no no fucking way

*(***FREE*** *tries to dismiss it.)*

FREE. [It was an accident, he misunderstood, you know my English sucks]

VIC. [Your English sucks?] That's [seriously] your excuse? This is fucking low. I mean, what the fuck, Free? Do [you hate me?]

FREE. [No! It was an accident – the guy got confused...]

MAGGIE. [Stop! What are you two talking about? Vic?]

VIC. *(to* **FREE***)* [Well. Shit. My Deaf lesbian sister seduced my boyfriend. That's never happened before.]

MAGGIE. [What?]

FREE. [It's just emails, it's no big deal]

VIC. [Just emails??] Not a big deal that [you're going behind my back with my boyfriend?] No big deal that [you're in love with my boyfriend?]

FREE. [I'm not in love with him! It was just words, late at night, just talk. I couldn't sleep.]

VIC. [So talk to Maggie!] That's what she's here for. You've already [got your lover. Why don't you talk to her? Huh?]

(silence)

Maggie?

(silence)

Hell, aren't you a [<u>dyke</u>]? You [<u>don't even like</u>]
Ram!

[<u>Just, don't do anything. Just don't! He's happy.
I'm happy. Leave us alone. Leave us the fuck
alone.</u>]

(VIC *exits.* **MAGGIE** *is stunned, starts to exit.)*

(Dialogue in ASL only, English on screen)

FREE. [Wait.]

MAGGIE. [No]

FREE. [Stay. Let's talk. This was no big deal. It was an
accident. It was no big deal.]

MAGGIE. [Not now]

FREE. [Come on, it was an accident. Let's talk! We
always talk about whatever is wrong…That's us,
communication, otherwise we fall apart.]

MAGGIE. [No. That's me. Communication. Have you
been talking to me, Free? Really? Have you?]

(MAGGIE *exits.)*

(FREE, *angry, signs to herself and the world.)*

FREE. [I have to talk to someone, don't I? Don't I?]
[Where the hell are you?]
[Fuck!]

(blackout)

Scene Four

(Lights up on **VIC***'s apartment.)*

*(***RAM*** is happy,* **VIC** *is alternately clingy and passive aggressive)*

*(***MAGGIE*** *interprets under the streetlight)**

VIC. Don't go

RAM. I have to. Actually, I'm excited.

VIC. Hey!

RAM. I am. I'm excited about work. I'm excited about everything.

VIC. Huh

RAM. What?

VIC. Well, I think that might be the first unromantic thing you've said to me all weekend

RAM. No it's not

VIC. What do you mean it's not? How is it not?

RAM. You're the reason I'm excited!

VIC. About leaving

RAM. I'm not leaving.

VIC. Then what?

RAM. I'm… continuing!

VIC. Continuing??

RAM. Continuing!

VIC. That's… Ok, what are you continuing? Continuing like… along your way?

RAM. What do you mean?

VIC. Well, I mean, it's not like I haven't seen people continuing before. Continuing right out of my life.

RAM. Nonononononono, that's leaving. I'm not leaving, I'm continuing.

VIC. Stop being so…! What's the fu –, – the difference?

*Optional stage direction

RAM. Continuing implies… implies the continuation of something

VIC. Oh, ok, thanks

RAM. No, listen. Continuing implies togetherness, not separation

VIC. According to you

RAM. According to me

VIC. Ok, so in the dictionary of Ram, what is getting on a plane and flying to another state?

RAM. That's geography

VIC. That's bull

RAM. That's crass

VIC. So is that why you're leaving? Because I'm crass?

RAM. Vic, come on. Are you serious?

VIC. Of course I'm serious! God! Aren't you listening to me?

RAM. Really?

VIC. Hell, I don't know. Serious about what? See? I don't even know what we're talking about. I'm dumb.

RAM. I can't leave you.

VIC. People do. Plenty do. Two husbands did, and without looking back

RAM. I'm sorry, I shouldn't have joked, I didn't think about that

VIC. You were joking?

RAM. Well no, but I was being flippant

VIC. Well, quit it! You know, girls need reassurance too

RAM. Alright wait

VIC. No, I'm just saying, I don't need it right now

RAM. Victoria. Quiet.

VIC. Victoria? Oh, no no, no one calls me that

RAM. Victoria? It suits you. You're strong and regal

VIC. Shut up

RAM. No, that's not true. You're warm. You're the warmest person I know. With depths that only I have seen. I think. Don't disillusion me if I'm wrong. I like to pretend you're my secret. That no other man has ever known you this way

VIC. Jealous much?

RAM. Absolutely. It's an Indian thing. We like our women untouched.

VIC. Well then you shouldn't touch them.

RAM. Why don't you like Victoria?

VIC. No one calls me that

RAM. Why not? It's your name.

VIC. I'm not very virginal.

RAM. What does that have to do with the price of eggs?

(**VIC** *puts her cards on the table, daring him to leave her.*)

VIC. First boy I had sex with, Brett, tells me afterwards that I can't call myself Victoria anymore because she was the virgin queen and I don't qualify now. Then he told all the other guys, and they changed my name to Vic. Did I mention I was fourteen? Fourteen and no longer Victoria. How does your Indian-ness feel about that?

RAM. I don't like him. Did you like him?

VIC. Loved him madly. Why?

RAM. He's an ass

VIC. Strong language, mr professor man

RAM. Victoria wasn't the virgin queen, that was Elizabeth.

(*beat*)

VIC. No shit?

RAM. No shit.

VIC. Asshole! Wait, weren't they both virgins?

RAM. It is generally assumed that Victoria's marriage was consummated.

VIC. What an asshole!

RAM. Completely undeserving of Victoria.

VIC. Yeah, well. Victoria was bored and 'something had to give'. And then there was Vic.

RAM. Do you like Vic?

VIC. Not really. That's what they call victims on crime shows.

(Feeling stupid, she continues to push him.)

Not that you watch TV… I really like TV, you should know that!

RAM. Why do you think I don't watch TV?

VIC. Maggie and Free don't even own a TV

RAM. Well, unlike your somewhat abrasive sister who doesn't like me, I watch TV

VIC. Really?

RAM. I'm Indian, we have a passionate relationship with mindless entertainment! I'll have to take you to a Bollywood film some time. Good guys, bad guys, romance, singing, the whole bit.

VIC. Dork

RAM. That's what I'm telling you. So what's this crime show that you watch?

VIC. There's like a million *Law and Order*'s, but I like the *CSI* shows

RAM. I will begin watching as soon as I get home.

(He's broken through.)

VIC. Familiarize yourself with the genre?

RAM. Absolutely. I can find out about all those other lesser Vics.

VIC. You know what, you're right. I never liked Vic. Vic has sex with pimply Brett and marries any asshole who proposes and Vic is drunk and pathetic. Fuck Vic.

RAM. Excellent. Victoria. I love you

VIC. Yeah?

RAM. And I'm not leaving, I'm continuing, because you're a part of me now and I have to go to work and then I have to come back and that's how we continue on. Together. You'll see. We won't stop talking, I promise. You'll see.

VIC. Ok.

RAM. Besides, it'll be fun.

VIC. How will it be fun, you lunatic?

RAM. Writing to each other again, lamplight and the tapping of a keyboard, I don't know how I ever survived without you...

(**VIC** *moves around, changes the subject.*)

VIC. Did you check around, make sure you didn't leave anything?

RAM. Like the first time?

VIC. Haha. Funny funny man, that's what I fell for, you know, that wacky sense of humor.

RAM. Really?

VIC. Get real. I'll look, Mom trained us well, I can spot a sock behind the radiator of a cheap motel room better than anyone. Never leave anything behind – no kids no luggage – that was her motto – like the marines only not – cuz marines do leave shit behind, like me for example...

(**RAM** *kisses her*)

RAM. Is this real enough for you.

VIC. Yes. But you have to call me.

RAM. I will

VIC. In the evening. Mornings are nice, but I like hearing your voice before I go to sleep. I sleep better.

RAM. It's a deal.

VIC. Alright. OK.

I'm done here.

Continue

RAM. Your majesty

> *(lights fade)*
>
> *(blackout)*
>
> *(on screen)*
>
> To: Jonesgirl
> From: Balaram
>
> Good evening, Victoria.
>
> *(Lights up on Free and Maggie's apartment.* **FREE** *checks her Blackberry,* **MAGGIE** *watches her.)*
>
> *(ASL on screen)*

FREE. [You don't have to watch me, I won't email him back.]

> To: Jonesgirl
> From: Balaram
>
> Are you there?
>
> *(They both read,* **MAGGIE** *signs.)*

MAGGIE. [If you screw this up for Vic I will not forgive you.]

FREE. [It was screwed up from the beginning. It was an accident.]

MAGGIE. [Stay out of it. They're making it work.]

> To: Jonesgirl
> From: Balaram
> Vic?
>
> *(***FREE** *puts aside the Blackberry, turns to* **MAGGIE.***)*

FREE. [Can we talk?]

MAGGIE. [No]

> *(Screen goes dark.* **MAGGIE** *exits.)*
>
> *(Lights fade on* **FREE.***)*
>
> *(Telephone rings. Lights up on* **VIC** *at the club. She's been waiting for this call, she braces herself,*

answers her cellphone. Lights up on **RAM**. *The club is noisy, so they have to yell.)*

(words on screen)

VIC. Hey baby! I'm so glad you called, the apartment was so lonely after you left I had to get out!

RAM. I wondered where you were, you didn't answer…

VIC. How was your flight?

RAM. Fine

VIC. What's happening tomorrow?

RAM. Isn't that the universal question

VIC. What?

RAM. I don't know. Actually, I don't care, that's more accurate.

VIC. Ram? What's wrong, sweetie?

RAM. Nothing. I'm hyperventilating.

VIC. Well, quit it. Do you have a paper bag?

RAM. Trust you to not take me too seriously. I love you, you know that Vic?

VIC. I love you

RAM. Ok, good. Then lets get married.

VIC. What?

RAM. I had a moment here, tonight. I thought I might not get to talk to you. And now I'm hyperventilating, it's ridiculous! So that settles it then. Please marry me.

–

Hello?

VIC. Yes.

RAM. Promise?

VIC. Yes!

(blackout)

PART IV

Scene 1

*(**RAM**'s V.O. in dark. Sanskrit on screen. Pool of light on **RAM** and **VIC** embracing.)*

Loo jurai, jurau!
    Vaanijjam hoi, hou tam nama
Ehi! Nimajjasu pase,
    Pupphavai! Na ei me nidda

*(Lights up on **MAGGIE** Interpreting under the street-light.)**

*(**RAM** and **VIC** in bed.)*

RAM. Now translated –
    Some will always be
    Unhappy
    Let them
    And some will
    Blame us
    Let them
    Alright you're having
    your period
    come and lie beside me
    anyway
    I can't sleep without you

    There!

VIC. I think that's romantic!

RAM. Most people laugh –

VIC. Oh whatever, most people are idiots. I love that!

*Optional stage direction

73

RAM. I do too!

It's in Prakrit, which is like a working class Sanskrit, not as refined, but this is part of who we are, yes? It shows a side of ancient India that westerners don't see, the Hindus were a very sexual people, and so often the eastern people are seen as uptight and puritanical when in fact it is the Americans who are puritanical. Who deride a woman for her sexuality instead of celebrating it

VIC. It's brilliant! It's like – 'Hey honey I'm on the rag, I can't,' and he's like 'I don't care, I just wanted to cuddle'

(**RAM** *starts to laugh.*)

What's funny? Is that not what it's saying?

RAM. No, that's exactly what it's saying

(**VIC** *jumps on* **RAM.**)

VIC. Then what's funny, mr. man?

RAM. Nothing, you're exactly right. It's just, I've always had a sort of adolescent response to that phrase –

VIC. What? On the rag?

What's wrong with it? 'On the rag... on the rag...' it's true –

RAM. Oh, certainly, accuracy is paramount in these matters

VIC. Well yeah, I suppose it sounds all beautiful and flowery in Sanskrit – 'On the raagaah' –

(**RAM** *loses it, he's falling over laughing.*)

RAM. – Oh my god!

VIC. Raga? Did I get it? Is that right? Raga!

RAM. Oh no no no no, stop, stop

VIC. What? Was I close?

RAM. No! No more Sanskrit from you, I beg of you!

(*He tries to roll away from her, and she rolls with him, needling him.*)

VIC. So how do you say it? That's what I'm calling it if you won't tell me.

Sorry honey, I can't, I'm on the 'raga'

RAM. You're killing me!

VIC. Tell me what it means! Tell me! Raga, raga, what does it mean –

RAM. Ok, Ok! Stop, stop, no more. Stop.

Song. It means song.

*(Something passes between them, he strokes her hair.)**

(**MAGGIE** *leaves the streetlight, finds her Yeats book, sits, opens it.*)

Raga

VIC. Song

(Lights fade on VIC *and* RAM. *Yeats poem appears on screen,* MAGGIE *murmurs a few lines quietly.* FREE *watches her.*)

MAGGIE.

When you are old and gray and full of sleep,
And nodding by the fire, take down this book,
And slowly read, and dream of the soft look
Your eyes had once, and of their shadows deep;

How many loved your moments of glad grace,
And loved your beauty with love false or true,
But one man loved the pilgrim soul in you,
And loved the sorrows of your changing face;

And bending down beside the glowing bars,
Murmur, a little sadly, how Love fled
And paced upon the mountains overhead
And hid his face among a crowd of stars.

(**FREE** *approaches,* **MAGGIE** *shuts the book.*)

(Poem disappears, ASL on screen.)

*Optional stage direction

FREE. [What are you reading?]

MAGGIE. [Just a poem]

(beat)

FREE. [Vic is happy]

MAGGIE. [You think someone should thank you for that?]

FREE. [Look, Vic has forgiven me, so why can't you?]

MAGGIE. [Vic hasn't forgiven you, she wants you at the wedding so she can keep an eye on you. She doesn't trust you.]

(beat)

FREE. [There's nothing to be jealous of. There was nothing between us, just words.]

MAGGIE. [I'm not jealous, Free. I'm just not ready to talk to you.]

FREE. [Fine. You're not jealous. So tell me why you're mad.]

MAGGIE. [Why am I mad? You walk around with a chip on your shoulder for months, making me feel like I'm doing something wrong, then you take your bitchiness out on your sister, lie to the man she loves on email, and you can ask me why I'm mad?]

FREE. [And that's it? You're not at all worried that maybe I have feelings for someone else? That maybe I'm in love with someone else?]

MAGGIE. [No! Through email? What is wrong with you?]

FREE. [Pay attention to me!!]

MAGGIE. [I am and you're not making sense!!]

FREE. [Then you're not listening!]

(beat)

MAGGIE. [Fine. Then try again. Try very hard to explain this so it makes sense to me, because I do not understand you.]

FREE. [Maybe you can't understand me anymore. Maybe we don't speak the same language.]

MAGGIE. [What?]

FREE. [Ok.]

[We were talking.]

[Remember that?]

[And then you started talking to someone else, in English. Not just someone else, lots of other people, and the conversation went on and on, and things changed as a result of this conversation, your work, your world, your life. And sometimes you talked to me too, but not as much, and this other conversation was so busy there was no time for other things, but I was still here, so that was ok.]

[But while you changed and moved and became all these new people, I waited. You see? I waited in the other language, the second language, for you to come back so we could continue. Continue our conversation. But you didn't. You went on and thought that I should keep up. But I can't keep up. I was waiting, and trying really hard not to change, so that when you returned we could... continue... But you didn't.]

[And then you were having your new conversation with my sister. You never used to be able to talk to my sister, that's how much you changed! And that's when I could see it! How far you'd gone without me. Or with the old me, while I did nothing. Nothing with my life!]

[So I needed to have a conversation. Ok? I needed to talk, and suddenly there it was, a conversation for me. As I am now, that I can have! So I did it.]

[Because you're not here anymore.]

(silence)

(**MAGGIE** *struggles to re-orient herself*)

MAGGIE. [Is that so bad...? That I talk to Vic...?]

FREE. [No! None of it is bad. It's just gone.]

[Did I say it better? This time? Do you understand?]

(*They stare at each other.*)

(*lights fade*)

(*blackout*)

Scene Two

(Lights up on **FREE** *going to bed on the couch. She lies awake for the duration of this scene.)*

(Sound of telephone ringing. Lights up on **RAM** *in a hotel room on the phone, booting up his laptop.)*

(words on screen)

RAM. Victoria? I'm in a hotel! No, I'm not drunk, but I think I have to stay here. I strongly suspect my cousins have posted a guard. They're apparently superstitious about weddings, but at least I think I persuaded them to let me get some sleep for tomorrow.

(Lights up on **VIC** *on the phone.)*

VIC. Poor baby

RAM. How are you?

VIC. I'm still packing, I know I know, but I'm almost done, swear! And then I'm gonna crash, I am not getting married with bags under my eyes and no hangover to show for it. Aw, that sucks though, are you gonna be lonely all by yourself?

RAM. No, no, I have my laptop, I'll get some work done.

VIC. Dork

RAM. I miss you

VIC. Always. It's just til tomorrow...

RAM. Can't wait.

(beat)

Victoria?

VIC. Hm?

RAM. Would you email me?

VIC. What? Silly –

What's wrong with the phone?

RAM. Nothing. I just … miss that

VIC. That's silly. I ah –

I don't know what you're talking about

Hold on, the phone is – just a sec –

*(**VIC** covers the mouthpiece of the phone for several breaths. Her heart is pounding.)*

(She finally decides to come almost clean.)

VIC. *(cont.)* Hi honey?

RAM. Yes

VIC. Ok, that's better – I was getting this wacky buzzing noise – What were you saying?

RAM. I just said send me an email –

VIC. Oh, honey, I just want to finish packing! Anyway, I haven't used my email in months, I don't even know if I'd remember my password –

(beat)

Ram?

RAM. Yeah

VIC. OK, that's it, last box. I'm really sleepy, ok honey? I'll see you in the morning

Sweet dreams

RAM. Yeah

(They hang up.)

*(**VIC** sits with the phone in her hand, wide awake, breathing.)*

*(**MAGGIE** appears in doorway and looks at **FREE**.)*

MAGGIE. [Good night]

*(**MAGGIE** exits.)*

(lights fade)

(blackout)

Scene Three

(Lights up on **MAGGIE** *and* **FREE** *waiting on a bench.* **FREE** *is on her Blackberry,* **MAGGIE** *glances over her shoulder.)*

(words on screen)

MAGGIE. [Solitaire?]

*(***FREE** *nods.* **MAGGIE** *points and signs.)*

[...Red queen]

*(***FREE** *keeps playing.)*

*(***RAM** *enters in a rush, computer bag in hand.)*

MAGGIE. [<u>Ram! Happy wedding day!</u>]

RAM./MAGGIE. [<u>Sorry I'm late!</u>]

MAGGIE. [<u>No, no, don't worry about it! Everyone's already inside, there's a coat check over there for your things, I'll go tell Vic you're here, she's almost ready –</u>]

*(***MAGGIE** *exits.)*

RAM. ok, thanks

FREE. [Hi]

RAM. Hi

FREE. [Congratulations]

RAM. Thanks

(He sits next to her on the bench, glances at the Blackberry.)

FREE. [Just killing time. Sorry.]

RAM. Oh no, go ahead, I don't mind

*(***FREE** *returns to her Blackberry.)*

*(***RAM** *takes out his laptop, opens it. He types, words on screen.)*

RAM. TO: jonesgirl
FROM: balaram

You must have thought I was an idiot

(The message pops up on **FREE** *'s blackberry. She freezes, looks around, considers leaving, finally looks at him, reads the message again, shakes her head, types.)*

TO: balaram
FROM: jonesgirl

vic loves you

(Both are careful not to look directly at the other as they continue typing. This is a secret conversation.)

TO: jonesgirl
FROM: balaram

You could have told me the truth at any time. You didn't.

(beat)

TO: balaram
FROM: jonesgirl

what will you do?

(beat)

TO: jonesgirl
FROM: balaram

Vic doesn't know about us. Don't tell her.

*(***FREE** *looks at him now, searches his face, realizes he means it.)*

(Relieved, she types.)

TO: balaram
FROM: jonesgirl

ok

(They both sit silently for a beat, then **FREE** *types.)*

I was lonely

RAM. Yeah well –

 TO: jonesgirl

 FROM: balaram

 I was lonely too. But I'm changing that.

 (silence.)

 We were lovers

 Do you realize that?

 *(**RAM** signs "you, me, lovers")*

 *(**RAM** hears voices offstage, gestures to **FREE.** **RAM** puts away his laptop, **FREE** conceals her blackberry, but the words 'we were lovers' linger on the screen.)*

 *(**MAGGIE** enters.)*

MAGGIE. [<u>OK, are you ready?</u>] Da, da – da – daaa – *('here comes the bride')*

 *(**VIC** enters, wearing an Indian wedding sari.)*

RAM. Hey! Look at you!

VIC. [<u>Yeah, your mom</u>] made me like a hospital bed, I feel like I'm going to [<u>unravel</u>] any minute, there's this [<u>one measly little pin right here,</u>] and then a lot of [<u>tucking – I'm babbling.</u>]
 [<u>It looks ok?</u>]

 *(**VIC** searches Ram's face.)*

FREE. [<u>You're beautiful</u>]

MAGGIE. [<u>You look like a queen</u>]

VIC. – Ram?

 (beat)

RAM./MAGGIE. [<u>Don't worry. If anything starts slipping I'll hang on to you</u>]

VIC. My hero!

 [<u>You OK</u>]? You look a little…

RAM./MAGGIE. [No! They had me drinking last night, I'm a bit dehydrated. Nothing marrying you won't fix.]

(to **FREE***)* [Free, since you're Victoria's only family here today, I just wanted to say – I'll take care of her. I'll make her happy.]

FREE./MAGGIE. [thank you]

RAM./MAGGIE. [I love that word you two use – lover, right? Great word.]

(to **VIC***)* [You are what you do]

VIC. Right

RAM./MAGGIE. [Right.]

[So, Victoria, let's do this.]

(**RAM** *takes* **VIC***'s hand.* **RAM***,* **VIC***, and* **MAGGIE** *exit.*)

(**FREE** *deletes the words remaining on Blackberry/screen.*)
(*Blackout with final letter.*)

Scene Four

(Lights up on **MAGGIE** *and* **FREE** *alone in their apartment, post-party.* **MAGGIE** *sits in the dark.)*

*(***FREE** *approaches, turns on a table lamp, illuminating their hands and faces.* **MAGGIE** *has been crying.)*

*(***FREE** *finds the Yeats book, returns and sits across from* **MAGGIE**.*)*

(ASL only, dialogue on screen.)

MAGGIE. [Oh, don't bother, you won't like it. I was a kid, it's just a poem – I don't care about it –]

*(***MAGGIE** *reaches for the book,* **FREE** *hangs on to it.)*

[Shit Free, what happened to us?]

*(***FREE** *keeps reading.)*

[OK.]

[Do you want me to translate?]

FREE. [No.]

(She puts the book down and faces **MAGGIE**.*)*

[When you're old, and gray]

MAGGIE. [Stop… I'm sorry…]

FREE. [Shut up. When you're old and gray, and falling asleep all the time, can't carry on a conversation, arthritis in your hands…]

MAGGIE. [I'm sorry, you were right –]

[I don't know what happened –]

FREE. [Maybe you'll need a book to communicate with me, you'll open it and point at words, and I'll bring you what you need]

MAGGIE. [You're not old?]

FREE. [I exercise more]

MAGGIE. [Ok]

FREE. [And people will talk, and say look at those old witches, what do they do all day, they can't even have a conversation, poor things!]

MAGGIE. [Well they're stupid]

FREE. [That's right. Because even though you have no period anymore, and you're old and wrinkly and almost dead, I just like having you next to me in bed. I can't sleep without you.]

MAGGIE. [Me too]

FREE. [Me too]

(When FREE joins their hands, the signs for 'me too' [same] become the word 'continue'.)

FREE. [Continue]

(Lights fade.)

End of Play

APPENDIX

Transcriptions of Sanskrit poems used in *Love Person* courtesy of David L. Gitomer, Ph.D., DePaul University.

Poem on page 9:

॥१॥

अविदितसुखदुःखं निर्गुणं वस्तु किञ्चित्
जडमतिरिह कश्चिन्मोक्ष इत्याचक्षसे ।
मम तु मतमनंगस्मेरतारुण्यघूर्णन्
मदकलमदिराक्षी विनिमोक्षो हि मोक्षः ॥

Poem on page 33:

॥२॥

किमपि किमपि मन्दं मन्दमासत्तियोगाद्
अविरलितकपोलं जल्पतोरक्रमेण ।
अशिथिलपरिरम्भव्यापृतैकैकदोष्णोर्
अविदितगतयामा रात्रिरेव व्यरंसीत् ॥

Poem on page 55:

॥३॥

जये धरित्र्या: पुरमेव सारम्
पुरे गृहं सद्मनि चैकदेश: ।
तत्रापि शय्या शयने वरस्त्री
रत्नोज्ज्वला राज्यसुखस्य सारम् ॥

Poem on page 75:

॥४॥

लोओ जुरे जुरौ!
वाणिज्जं होइ होउ तं नाम।
एहि! निमज्जसु पासे
पुप्फवै! न एइ मे निद्दा ॥

THE HOUSE OF BLUE LEAVES
John Guare

Farce / 4m, 6f / Interior

Artie Shaugnessy is a songwriter with visions of glory. Toi ng by day as a zoo-keeper, he suffers in seedy lounges by night, ing his wares at piano bars in Queens, New York where he lives ith his wife, Bananas. Artie's downstairs mistress, Bunny Fli us will sleep with him anytime but refuses to cook until they e married. On the day the Pope is making his first visit to the c , Artie's son Ronny goes AWOL from Fort Dix stowing a hom. made-bomb intended to blow up the Pope in Yankee Stadium Also arriving is Artie's old school chum, now a successful Hollywood producer, Billy Einhorn with starlet girlfriend in tow, who holds the key to Artie's dreams of getting out of Queens and away from the life he so despises. But like many dreams, this promise of glory evaporates amid the chaos of ordinary lives.

"Enchantingly zany and original farce."
– *The New York Times*

GLENGARRY GLEN ROSS
David Mamet

Dramatic Comedy / 7m / 2 Interiors

This scalding comedy took Broadway and London by storm and won the 1984 Pulitzer Prize. Here is Mamet at his very best, writing about small-time, cutthroat real estate salesmen trying to grind out a living by pushing plots of land on reluctant buyers in a never-ending scramble for their share of the American dream. Revived on Broadway in 2006 this masterpiece of American drama became a celebrated film which starred Al Pacino, Jack Lemmon, Alec Baldwin and Alan Arkin.

"Crackling tension... ferocious comedy and drama."
– *New York Times*

"Wonderfully funny... A play to see, remember and cherish."
– *New York Post*

OTHER TITLES AVAILABLE FROM SAMUEL FRENCH

GETTING AND SPENDING
Michael J. Chepiga

Dramatic Comedy / 4m, 3f

A brilliant and beautiful investment banker makes illegal profits of eighteen million dollars from insider trading and uses it to build housing for the homeless. Shortly before her trial, she ferrets out the foremost criminal attorney of the era to persuade him to abandon his retirement in a Kentucky monastery to defend her. This play is about them: their struggles with themselves, with each other, with the law and with her unusual defense.

"Stirs the conscience while entertaining the spirit."
— *Los Angeles Times*

"An off beat, audacious comedy, well worth seeing."
— *WNBC TV*

OTHER TITLES AVAILABLE FROM SAMUEL FRENCH

THE DOWNSIDE
Richard Dresser

Comedy / 6m, 2f / Combined Interior

American business is the target of this hilarious and cutting satire originally produced at Long Wharf Theatre. A pharmaceutical firm has acquired rights to market a European anti stress drug and marketing has got to come up with a snazzy ad campaign. Nowhere is this drug more needed than right here at Mark & Maxwell to counter corporate ineptitude. The strategy meetings get more pointless and frenetic as the deadline approaches. These meetings are chaired by Dave who is never actually there; he is a voice directing the campaign from his mobile phone while jetting between meetings, unstoppable even when his plane is hijacked.

"Funny and ruthlessly cynical."
– *Philadelphia Inquirer*

"Sheer delight."
– *Westport News*